JEWISH COMMUNITIES
BOHEMIA-MORAVIA
(See inside back cover for list)

I am a
holocaust torah

I am a
holocaust torah

The Story of the Saving of 1,564 Torahs Stolen by the Nazis

Rabbi **Alex J. Goldman**

gefen גפן
publishing house בית הוצאת לאור
JERUSALEM ◆ NEW YORK

Pagination & Graphic Design: Studio Paz, Jerusalem
Illustrator: Susanne Berger
Photography: Mel Abfier

2 4 6 8 9 7 5 3

Gefen Publishing House
6 Hatzvi St., Jerusalem, 94386, Israel
972-2-538-0247 • orders@gefenpublishing.com

Gefen Books
600 Broadway, Lynbrook, NY 11563, USA
516-593-1234 • orders@gefenpublishing.com

www.israelbooks.com

www.czechtorah.org

Printed in Israel

Send for our free catalogue

ISBN 965-229-236-2

Library of Congress Cataloging-in-Publication Data:

Goldman, Alex J.

I am a Holocaust Torah: The story of 1,564 Torahs stolen by Nazis from synagogues
in Czechoslovakia, rescued twenty years later, and placed in the hands of people who
love them.

1. Holocaust, Jewish (1939-1945) – Juvenile Fiction.

[1. Holocaust, Jewish (1939-1945) Fiction. 2. Torah scrolls -Fiction.] I. Title

PZ7.G5678 Ian 2000 • [Fic]-dc21 • CIP Number: 99-053815

INTRODUCTION

The Holocaust began on November 9, 1938, when the Nazis in Germany began to destroy the Jewish community. The night is called Kristallnacht, which means the "Night of Glass" or the "Night of Broken Glass." Synagogues were bombed and burned; Jewish books, prayer books and Talmuds were thrown into huge bonfires; many valuable religious objects were carried away; and Jewish-owned stores were looted.

The Holocaust spread to every country in Europe. Ghettos and concentration camps were established where hundreds of thousands of Jews were sent to die. Six million Jews died during the years of the Holocaust.

The story of *I Am a Holocaust Torah* began in Czechoslovakia. The Nazis took over the country. They roared into smaller states like Moravia and Bohemia, destroying synagogues, and carrying Torahs and Torah adornments, such as the crowns, breastplates and mantles, back to Prague, the country's capital.

By 1944, the *1,564 Torahs* and many adornments had been gathered.

The war ended in 1945, but the Torahs remained in Prague, forgotten.

Twenty years later, in 1964, an English art dealer negotiated with the Czech authorities to take the Torahs out of the country to London. An English Jewish philanthropist paid all the expenses for the transfer. The Torahs were brought to Westminster Synagogue and examined by *sofrim* ("scribes"). Both those fit for use, or kosher (which means that they could be read from), and those unfit for use, or non-kosher, would be sent to synagogues and other institutions that asked for them. They would be sent only on loan. The Torahs would not be sold, because they belong to the Jewish people.

More than 1,000 Torahs have found homes throughout the world. Those that remain are part of a permanent exhibit at the Czech Memorial Scrolls Center in Kent House of Westminster Synagogue, London.

I Am a Holocaust Torah is the historic and dramatic story of the *1,564 Torahs* through the mind, heart and words of a Torah.

Alex J. Goldman
Stamford, Connecticut, 2000

The Torah is a tree of life to those who hold her firmly.

Prayer book

Some scrolls live fortunate, happy lives.
They are carried around during services. . . .
Rabbis dance, holding them aloft. Other scrolls are
unlucky, pushed to the back of the ark, unloved,
silent. Still other scrolls suffer a tragic
fate and go through fire and suffering, die, or
survive in a damaged condition. Yet, all
contain the same sacred words, all are holy in
the eye of the beholder.

Those responsible for the Czech scrolls have perceived that the last survivors
still deserve their place in life, that they are witnesses who must stay alive
in order to be heard. And so they still live, not only at Kent House but
throughout the world where communities have received memorial scrolls
to show that the Torah does not disappear, that it must be heard.

Rabbi Albert H. Friedlander
Minister, Westminster Synagogue
Kent House, Knightsbridge
London

Respect this Torah, and behold that those people who
used to listen to the readings from the Torah in synagogues
were God-fearing Jews, honorable men and women
who longed to know the words of God and to walk
the path God prescribed in the Torah.
We believe that we are *Am Olam* -
an eternal people which will never perish.

When the cantor of Kolin took the Torah out of the Holy Ark,
he sang the opening lines of the Shema at the top of his voice.
These are the very same words which your chazan will sing,
a confession of faith which will unite you with our forefathers
and with our brothers and sisters,
whether they live east or west, north or south.

You have founded a new congregation, and I wish from the bottom of my heart that
it should flourish and that it should be the bearer of the idea of
brotherhood and peace for all peoples and nations.

Rabbi Dr. Richard Feder[*] (1875-1970)
On the Occasion of inauguration of a new
congregation after the Holocaust

[*] Dr. Richard Feder was the Rabbi of Kolin before the Holocaust in which he lost his entire family
and returned as an only survivor. In 1953 he was appointed Chief Rabbi of Czechoslovakia.

I am a Torah.
Not very large or small.
Medium-sized.

Some Torahs are new, fresh and clean, just recently prepared from sheepskin for writing on by a scribe, who is called a *sofer*. Fresh and clean. A sofer is a specialist, a religious man who has studied all the laws about how and with what to write a Torah -- what tools to use, the kind of ink and how it is prepared, the kind of parchment to use or not to use, the string or gut used to tie the folios together, and the quill with which to actually write the words. He also has to know about the columns -- how many, how to begin each one -- the spaces, and the precise number of letters on each line.

Some Torahs are old -- prepared years, often centuries
ago in different countries and continents.
Some were written in Israel where
there are special schools
for *sofrim*.

I am very, very old. I was very tired. Now I am alive again.

Some Torahs are more handsome than others, depending on the script created by the sensitive, loving, religious hand that carefully and lovingly stroked the letters onto the parchment.

I used to be handsome. No more! Now I have scars, burns, tears. Part of me is waterlogged. I was not kept dry.

You see, *I am a Holocaust Torah*, old and battered -- but still holy.

I come from Prague, Czechoslovakia, where I spent twenty years after the Nazis kidnapped and captured me from my hometown, Kosova Hora.

Kosova Hora, about twenty-five miles from Prague, was, like many towns and villages in Bohemia and Moravia, very small. In 1570, four hundred years ago, there were only two Jewish families there. A hundred years later, there were eighteen, or *chai*, Jewish families.

This meant that a synagogue had to be built and a cemetery established. There had to be a rabbi, *hazzan, shochet, mohel* and *sofer*, who would serve the small Jewish community.

We were fortunate because Reb Dovid'l, a handsome man with fiery blue eyes and a beautiful black beard, was a very gentle man. His every act was one of love and kindness. When he chanted, his voice rang melodically throughout the small wooden synagogue, thrilling the congregation, making the people feel very good. When he spoke from the pulpit, his message was always inspiring. He did not chastise, reprimand or insult anyone.

When he conducted a circumcision, which was not often, because of the size of our community, he performed the *mitzvah* with such love that the parents of the infant boy were not anxious as he brought the child into the covenant of Abraham.

When Reb Dovid'l chanted from the Torah on Shabbat and holidays, he enunciated each word clearly. When he corrected a Torah -- as when a letter could no longer be read clearly -- we could see in his eyes and hand the spirit of God guiding him.

We watched, fascinated, as he held the goose quill in his warm, soft hand, dipped it into the ink he had himself prepared, stretched out his arm, bent over the parchment -- his eyes intent, prayers quivering on his lips -- and urged the quill to create Hebrew letters.

11

When the community decided to write a complete new Torah (which became me), he carefully selected the parchment and ascertained its resilience and texture before his excited eyes smiled, "Yes."

So I was born.

I remember the first time I felt myself -- almost literally -- moved and touched, developing. It was the day after *Simchat Torah*. There was great excitement in the air as every member of the community came to the synagogue. Looking like a prophet, Reb Dovid'l sat in front of a table on the pulpit. A large *talit* enveloped his broad shoulders. The elders stood around him, waiting. Women with tears in their eyes watched from their gallery. Children sensed that something great was going to happen.

When Reb Dovid'l nodded that he was ready to begin -- to begin with the word *b'rayshit*, "in the beginning," his hand trembled. I could feel him quiver as he drew the rounded letter bet upon me. I could hear heavy breathing and feel the relaxation when someone began to sing, *Siman tov u-mazal tov*, "[Would that this be] good sign, good luck." Everyone joined in. I, a new Torah, was begun. I was on my way. Reb Dovid'l wrote a few more words on me and the celebration erupted in joyous frenzy.

Every day Reb Dovid'l spent a limited number of hours writing the Torah. He had to comply with Jewish law. And there are hundreds of laws about writing a Torah -- the appropriate materials, attitude, concentration, even feeling. Reb Dovid'l considered this a very serious mitzvah.

Each day, each week, as he progressed, he proudly showed off his work. People nodded and smiled. Until the last day, when all was finished except for the last few words. This meant another celebration, called *siyum*, "conclusion," when leaders of the community were given the honor of writing a letter or word under Reb Dovidl's careful and trained scrutiny.

When Reb Dovid'l wrote the last word of the Torah, *Yisrael* ("Israel"), the celebration exploded, and happiness was visible on everyone's face. No one held back the joy -- a Torah, God's unique gift to the Jewish people, was finished.

I was born.

I was a full-fledged Torah -- complete, beautiful, handsome and proud. And I shared that pride every Shabbat, and every Monday and Thursday when the Torah is read and each one called touches me with a *talit*. When I heard the chanting -- in loud, strong, voices -- of the blessings of the ages, I could hardly contain myself. I looked forward to every *Shabbat* just to confirm my importance. I was the center of their lives. Even when I was placed in the Holy Ark where it was dark, I could hear the people praying. I could hear Reb Dovid'l preaching and talking about me -- my lines, my words, my paragraphs, my stories and my ideas. I felt good.

Our community grew. More Jewish people moved in. Reb Dovid'l had to write another Torah. I did not mind. I was the first, the *b'chor*. This was honor enough for me. Over the years, Jewish people in small towns nearby arranged to spend the *Shabbat* in Kosova Hora, and we grew and grew.

Our little community remained strong, with other rabbis following Reb Dovid'l and his successors. We were blessed with every rabbi who led us through the phases of Jewish life. Changes were made. People celebrated weddings and *bar mitzvahs* and the birth of children. My Torah colleagues and I remained the same. We never changed.

Once in a while, I could feel a *sofer* opening me and looking at me and my thousands of letters -- to confirm that I was perfect, readable, chantable. The reading of me, the *Torah*, had to be perfect, without fault or blemish. I tried to remain still in the Holy Ark so as not to rub out my letters. I was happy. I was protected by a wrapper that held me tight and straight. An embroidered dress -- cut and prepared by the women -- kept me warm.

I remember the women describing the pattern on this dress: two lions of Judah surrounding and protecting the Ten Commandments. Above the lions was a *keter*, or "crown."

Then, suddenly, everything changed. We began to hear rumors about Jews. I had experienced this kind of thing in the seventeenth, eighteenth and nineteenth centuries. But in the twentieth century? It was hard to believe. But beginning in the late thirties, we heard that Germans who called themselves Nazis had decided to cleanse our beloved country of Jews.

We heard about Kristallnacht, wherein the synagogues in Germany were set afire -- along with many books, Bibles, prayer books and Talmuds. The rumors persisted. We heard predictions that no one would survive. Every Jew would be killed or exiled. Not even small towns would be exempted. In nearby villages like Zivohost detention camps were set up.

And a memorial service was held in Kosova Hora after the rabbi heard that a mass grave in Olbramovice now held the corpses of eighty-two prisoners who had been in a railroad transport. When I was taken out from the ark, carried and placed on the table to be read, I heard the news of the day. There was a lot of talk about escaping to the United States, to England, or even to China. I understood that many families were making plans to escape.

One of the issues I heard people talking about was what to do with the synagogue. They agreed that while the synagogue was a holy place of prayer, it was not as important as the Torahs. Synagogues could be destroyed and rebuilt, but Torahs, if defiled, remained defiled.

So plans were made -- I heard them while on the Torah table -- to stealthily take us out one night after dark – to other communities across the borders and into Russia or Poland. I was frightened. I did not want to be hurt. I was, after all, God's gift to the Jewish people.

The Nazis, who had made Czechoslovakia a protectorate, quickly understood that something was going on. One night, as darkness fell, a company of Nazis -- young blond men in uniforms, swastikas on their shirts and the arms of their jackets -- swept into Kosova Hora. They had known where the synagogue and the Torahs were. I could feel terror in my letters and spaces. When the ark doors were flung open and two strong, firm hands grabbed me -- as if I were some unholy object -- and pulled me out of my comfortable berth, I called out, "You can't do this to me! I am a Torah. I am God's treasure." But no one heard me.

"Here," one soldier commanded another, "here, take this, put it in the trunk. There must be others." I was furious. Calling me "it"? I was taken out and almost thrown onto the floor of the truck. I was bruised, I know, but I controlled myself. In minutes, four or five other Torahs joined me. We all looked at each other in disbelief.

"How dare they?" I asked.

My friend shushed me. "Be careful or they'll kill us, cut us up."

We bounced up and down on the van floor as we traversed the bumpy road. The crowns and breastplates, which had also been thrown into the truck, clanged, making a lot of noise. We were convinced that these soldiers were evil men. What had we ever done to them? The journey took an hour or so, whereupon the four or five of us were again picked up.

I couldn't see clearly, but before I knew it, after a jarring walk on hard concrete, I was thrown down onto a hard bench. My friends, the other Torahs, felt the same way: Such disrespect! Such dishonor!
Shame! Shame!

We could hear a heavy door bang closed. Then it was dark. Dank. We shivered. We wondered if we would be saved. Would God hear our cry?
Every day -- every morning, and all day long -- we asked these questions again and again.

No answer came. We became accustomed to the darkness and dankness. We talked, even as we lay on our sides. We told each other the stories that were written on us -- of Abraham, Isaac, and Jacob, of Sarah, Rebecca, Rachel and Leah, and of Joseph.

We repeated the stories of Moses -- of the crossing of the Red Sea and of the Ten Commandments. We took turns reminding ourselves of the wonderful messages in the Torah about a loving God, about loving one's neighbor and helping people, and about our longing for the Promised Land.

This constant dialogue kept us hopeful. We did not realize that twenty years had passed. It was now 1964, according to my calculations. We had slept so long.

Then, suddenly, we began to hear voices. What was going on? Were we going to be remembered? After all these years? The voices sounded closer and closer. I could hear English, a clipped English accent. I had never heard this accent, but I knew it was different. Was this a new breed? New Jews? Were the old Jews I'd known no longer interested or concerned? No longer alive? We stretched our wooden holders, like ears, to hear a bit, a morsel perhaps.

As the mumbled and muffled voices became clearer, we heard someone say that there were 1,564 of us, *1,564 Torahs*. He had not known the number, only that we had all been packed together, for warmth I'd thought. I could not even remember that so many had been squeezed in with us. During our captivity, it had become increasingly difficult to think. Now it was hard to remember.

I thought, "God! So many of us! Does this mean that many small towns like ours were destroyed? What happened to all the rabbis and cantors and scribes and Jews?" We touched each other to spread the news. At one point one evening we all cried. Do you know what it is to hear *1,564 Torahs* cry at once? It was a symphony of weeping.

We waited. Hope through tears became our emotion and prayer. One day I felt light! Yes, it was light! I tried to shield the brightness, but I wanted to see the light, the light I had been dreaming of for twenty years. I saw two men looking at us. I nudged the other Torahs.

"Here they are,"
one man said. His accent was Czech.

After a pause, the other man commented, "Incredible! They look so forlorn!
Packed like sardines." He turned around and we heard him crying. We
were touched.

"He's a friend," I whispered.
My neighbor touched me, saying, "Yes, yes, he's a friend."
It was quiet for a few moments, but it felt like an eternity.

The weeping man turned around and said to the Czech, "Yes, we will take them. All of them. We will fix them up, correct them, wash them, ready them for their destined role. It will take time. But we are committed."

"All of them?" the Czech asked.

"Yes, all. None will remain here. We will take them to England. To London. We have a friend who has said he will pay whatever it costs to transport them. He only insisted that these Torahs, after their wounds are healed, must never be sold. They will be sent around the world, to synagogues and other institutions, as memorials of the Holocaust. The world will learn again that Torahs cannot be destroyed."

We could hardly contain our excitement.

"God," I cried, "when?"

The man did not answer. He looked at all of us, then at me. We could see tears in his eyes. We knew that the time of our exile was over. We jostled each other. We laughed and we wept.

Time was no longer important. We could be patient now and wait. Time passed. In a month -- we'd counted -- early one morning, we heard many, many feet shuffling nearby. Something was happening! Something big and important. Then it happened. The door opened wide. It was removed, and we could hear the rusty hinges breaking. It was suddenly so bright that our eyes hurt. But we did not mind, for it was the light of hope.

Led by a man who reminded me of Reb Dovid'l, eight or nine people entered the room. The leader looked at us and grabbed his heart, as if he was suddenly feeling a sharp pain. He breathed deeply for a few moments, frozen in his tracks. He could not move.

Recovering, his voice shaking, he ordered: "Take them slowly, one at a time, wrap each one in new cloth, and gently, please, please, gently, place them in the lorries. Careful now. They are precious." We wait. I wait. Someone slips his hands under me and slowly raises me up and out. God, I am moving.

The air seems so clean. My letters and spaces dry out quickly. I feel myself being transported out of confinement -- along a path, down stairs, through double doors, eased onto a soft base, and covered with a blanket. I remember the number 1,564. How long will I have to wait? No matter. A little more time will not matter.

"Where are my crown, my breastplate, my *yad*?" I call. Then I hear a clanging. I smile. It would take days before we were prepared for the trip to -- where had he said? -- England? Where was England? It did not matter. We were free. Free at last, free at last.

Tired, exhausted, we slept during the journey, which took a few days.

I remember, as we were moved into another lorry, seeing the date, February 7, 1964. The streets were clean and wide. Parks were covered with snow.

We heard rain trickling, fresh water. But we did not become wet. It was refreshing to hear the patter of rain, as if we were being washed, cleansed. The lorry stopped. Are we here? Where is here? We see a large, imposing old building. I see the words "Kent House."

"Kent House?" I ask my neighbor. He shrugs his shoulders. Other words appear on a plaque on the side of the beautiful building. Since I am a creation of words, I make out the words -- "Westminster Synagogue, Knightsbridge, London." It looks so different from the little wooden synagogue I remember in Kosova Hora, the little synagogue that had been the center of a town of twenty-five houses.

Again, we are carried, one by one. I am second this time. I do not mind. I feel like I am coming home -- a temporary home, perhaps, but home nonetheless. I sense myself being lifted, raised high and carried. I am laid down slowly, carefully. Soon I feel rested. It is dry and bright and we are all together -- on different levels, but together, close. In front of me I see a number. What is this number? Is it like the tattooed numbers on the arms of Holocaust survivors?

I hear a woman's voice explain, "Each Torah has a number on its *etz chaim,* or "wooden holder," which corresponds to the number on the shelf; this is how we identify each one. We will study each Torah and find out where it comes from. My number is 1,272, matching the number on the shelf, my shelf -- my dry, clean shelf, my home, at least for now, which I happily share with others.

It does not take long for people to begin visiting. They look at us, smile, and occasionally shed a tear. Each of us is taken up individually. I can feel myself being lifted. I look up and see a distinguished-looking, gentle-faced man with a beard and head-covering staring at me. I feel him carrying me. It hurts to be moved. My whole body feels like it is tearing. After all, I had been cramped and bound for twenty years.

But the man is very careful. He moves me ever so slowly and lays me down on a long table. His soft hands open me. He looks and ponders, from the first column on the right side to the other columns. I can see his eyes searching.

I see his face turn white.

"What is it?" I ask. He does not hear me.

Another man approaches. "He's been hurt, Chaim." This man also examines me, and he says, "Cut, a little torn, but I think we can fix him up. Heal him. He will be kosher. Some synagogue will be able to read from him. Yes, yes! I am sure."

I cry, "Thank God! I will be whole again." I look at my neighbor who is a little taller than me. He is on a nearby table. His tears are flowing.

"They can't correct me," he says tearfully. "I've been damaged too much. They told me -- I mean, they said to each other -- that I will be a symbol of memorial, of remembering, like a *Kaddish*. That I will be placed in a special display case where people can look at me and remember the six million of our people who were killed."

34

"I am glad," I say. "We both will bear witness for our people. Who knows where we will be sent. I am sure I am not going back to Kosova Hora. I am sure Kosova Hora no longer exists. We will be sent to synagogues in other countries all over the world, each of us separately."

Two months pass. I am at peace. I am full of hope. I hear people approaching our room. I am as excited as I have ever been. I feel something deep in my heart and on my parchment. My words are bouncing, the dots and letters jumping with joy. What can it be? I wonder.

The door opens. I look hard and see a man who looks like a rabbi. He doesn't have a beard like Reb Dovid'l, but he looks like a rabbi. His face is clean-shaven and round, his cheeks ruddy. He is wearing a beautiful, colorful *kippa*. His eyes are searching. I can see his chest moving. The woman who has entered with him is a handsome woman, tall and dignified, with peppered hair swept back into a bun. She points to me.

"This one is from Kosova Hora, a little town not far from Prague. He was born (I hear the words) about three hundred years ago. He has been through so much -- so many generations -- held by so many, touched by men, women, and children. He's a treasure, a priceless treasure. His number is 1,272."

Her companion looks at me, then back to her, and says, "Yes, yes. May I take this Torah with me? Now?"

He waits.

"Yes, you may take this Torah with you to your synagogue. But remember, it belongs to the Jewish people, like all the others. You will look at this Torah and remember our faith and our heritage, and our people will live.

Always remember, the parchment may burn but the letters of the Torah can never be destroyed. They are part of God and God cannot be destroyed. "

Nervously, the young rabbi picks me up. He embraces me, kisses me and holds me tight. I can feel his heart beating and his fingers and hands quivering and moist.

Inside, I feel myself crying.

The rabbi looks at the woman, his eyes tearing, and says, "The Torah is crying tears of joy."

Following page: list of Jewish Communities
of Bohemia and Moravia in alphabetical order
(see inside front cover for location on map)

1	Batelov	31	Golčův Jeníkov	61	Liberec
2	Bechyně	32	Havlíčuv Brod	62	Libochovice
3	Běleč	33	Heřmanův Městec	63	Lipník Nad Bečvou
4	Benesov	34	Hluboká Nad Vlatouv	64	Liteň
5	Blevice	35	Hodonin	65	Lomnice
6	Boskovice	36	Holesov	66	Loštice
7	Brandýs Nad Labem	37	Hořepnik	67	Louny
8	Brno	38	Hořice	68	Luže
9	Brtnice	39	Hořovice	69	Malešov
10	Brumov	40	Hradec Králové	70	Mariánské Lázně
11	Břenzince	41	Hranice	71	Mělník
12	Bzenec	42	Hroubovice	72	Mikulov
13	Čáslav	43	Humpolec	73	Milevsko
14	Česká Lípa	44	Cheb	74	Mirotice
15	Českě Budějovice	45	Ivančice	75	Mladá Boleslav
16	Český Krumlov	46	Jevíčko	76	Moravský
17	Český Těšín	47	Jičín	77	Mořina
18	Čkyně	48	Jihlava	78	Myslkovice
19	Děčín	49	Jindřichův Hradec	79	Nová Cerekev
20	Divišov	50	Karlovy Vary	80	Nový Bydžov
21	Dlouhá Ves	51	Kasejovice	81	Olomouc
22	Dobruška	52	Kdyně	82	Opava
23	Dobriš	53	Kladno	83	Osoblaha
24	Doulní Kounice	54	Kojetín	84	Ostrava
25	Domažlice	55	Kolín	85	Pardubice
26	Doudleby Nad Orlicí	56	Kolinec	86	Plzeň
27	Dražkov	57	Kosova Hora	87	Podbřezí
28	Drmoul	58	Kostelec U Křízků	88	Poděbrady
29	Dřevíkov	59	Krnov	89	Podivín
30	Frýdek-Místek	60	Kroměříz	90	Pohořelice